The Final Entries
of J.H. Henning

Charlie Williams

For Sharon Rosenblatt, who encouraged me and taught me to love English class, no easy feat, I assure you.

1

The silence of a cold, pre-winter evening in a Manhattan apartment building was broken as the door to the famed author James Henry Henning's apartment fell with a crash to the floor as police swarmed in. Behind the blue-clad officers strode head detective Steve Osborn, his face grave, and his hand resting on the butt of his gun, sitting in its holster. For days, Henning's door had remained closed, and no noise at all could be heard from behind it. That, along with a recent murder in the area, had forced the authorities to take action.

"If you meet Henning, do not apprehend him by force unless he puts up a fight! Let's get this done as quickly as possible," Osborn called to his men.

Osborn entered Henning's living room, and allowed an amused smile to play across his leathery, mustached face. The walls around the room were crammed with books, most of them bearing titles of horror. Of course, that was Henning's specialty. For almost four years, the author had thrilled his readers with tales of fear and suspense. Which was why it had been such a surprise when he seemingly disappeared off the map almost a week ago. Even Henning's girlfriend had not seen a sign of him since then.

Turning back to the books, Osborn noticed something. The detective reached out and wiped his finger along the spine of a leather-bound volume. His finger came back covered in dust. Taking a closer look at the other books, he saw they were all covered in dust.

Something was wrong.

Henning hadn't used this room for some time. The books were untouched, and as he looked around, Osborn noticed other details about the room. The armchair in the corner had peculiar scratches along the arms, and the dark wooden coffee table in the middle of the room was also cloaked in dust.

Osborn exited the living room and ran into an ashen faced officer by the name of John Rosen. To Osborn's recollection, Rosen had served on the police force for five years. Never had Osborn seen such an expression of fear and shock on the face of a hardened officer. Rosen's features were contorted in a grimace, as if in pain, as he said, "We found Henning."

Osborn followed Rosen out of the room and down a narrow hallway. The same scratch marks that marred the armchair were trailed along the walls of the hall, until it opened into another room. Osborn entered it so quickly that he almost tripped over Henning's body.

The author was lying on his back, his eyes glazed over and unseeing. Protruding from his chest was a rounded piece of wood about as long as Osborn's arm, splattered with dried blood and shattered bone. The tip of the stake went clean through Henning, coming out of his back, caked with blood. The color had long since left Henning's features; the peculiar scarlet color of his eyes stood out on his bone white face. His body was completely still and limp, and Osborn didn't have to be a doctor to know that Henning had been dead for a while. The smell told him that.

"Clear the area," Osborn said. He was aware that his voice was trembling. "Get the body out of here, and look for evidence."

"This is an obvious murder." said a new cop on the force, standing in a corner of the room, as far away from the body as she could be from the corpse. "I would say we have all the evidence we need." Osborn shook his head.

"There's always something else," he explained. "If anything, trace for fingerprints on the stake. Don't leave this apartment without at least one…"

His voice trailed away. Squatting down, Osborn picked up a small, navy-blue book from the floor. It had caught his attention because it was the only volume in the apartment that wasn't covered in dust. As Osborn opened to the first page of the book, a note fell out. He caught it as it fluttered to the ground.

To Whom It May Concern:

By the time you find this letter, I will already be dead. Believe me, it is for the best. I am no longer a danger to myself and to those around me. This letter is enclosed in my diary. Read it if you want answers to what has happened to me. But be warned: you will not believe any of it at first. The experiences that led me to

this act are none for the faint of heart, and I beg for you
to understand my decision. After you read my final
writings, all will be made clear. Do not pity me in my
plight, in doing this act I save the lives of all who live in
New York City.

If you are reading this, and you are not Maria
Bennet, please see that this letter and the news of my
death reach her. Give her all of my love.

James Henry Henning

Osborn read the note over again, then put it back inside the diary. Then and there he made a decision, that, under other circumstances, he wouldn't have even considered. Looking around to make sure he was not being watched, Osborn slipped the diary into his coat pocket. Perhaps he would regret doing it later, but at the moment, curiosity had completely overtaken him.

After overseeing the removal of Henning's body, Osborn left the apartment building ahead of his officers, and immediately headed straight for the police station as a blood-red sun set on New York City.

. . .

Bourbon glowed gold in the glass in Steve's hand as he settled back in his chair and took a swig. The window outside his second story apartment looked out on a dark, lamp-lit night as a light snow started to fall. Taking in the view of last-minute dog walkers and swirling snowflakes, he propped his feet up on his desk, opened the small, dark blue diary, and began to read.

2

It is well known among the public that I write in a most peculiar fashion. While other authors may choose to brainstorm ideas for new novels in the comfort of their homes, in front of glowing laptop screens, I choose to travel worldwide for the perfect real-life setting to start my latest book.

Which is exactly why I chose to take a trip to Romania, former home of the infamous Vlad III of Wallachia, better known to the public as Vlad Dracula.

Yes, my books had always been best sellers, but while writing novels about ghouls and werewolves were a hit with my audience, what they were clamoring for these days were *vampires*, those undead beings that stalk the night in search of human blood. Strangely, I had not written a novel on vampires up until this point. Perhaps it was because of my disgust at reading the overly romantic Twilight series, but I had avoided the topic of vampires since the start of my writing career.

Fortunately for me, Romania offered many a vampire lore for me to elaborate on. That was how I found myself in a crowded airport in Budapest, jostled by fellow travelers towards the exit, where cabs would take them to lavish hotels. Unlike them, however, a place of rest and relaxation was not my destination.

Over the years, I had found that for my reader to experience the terror and fear in my novels, I had to experience it first. This time I was packed for a camping trip; I would spend the night in the immense Black Forest of Wallachia, waiting for my imagination to possess me, thus springing my new novel from my head.

For me, it is not really the character that is always key to the story, but the setting. One simply cannot have horror story when there is sunshine and rainbows in a clear blue sky, and a bunny is hopping through the woods. Unless, of course, the bunny is rabid. Then it can get rather freaky.

Ah, I'm getting off topic again. I bought this diary to record my trip, but I seem to write every word that pops into my head on its pages. I'll try to regulate that.

Anyway, the taxi dropped me at the campsite just as the sun was setting. Perfect. Dusk was the best time for shadows to cast an eerie light over my surroundings. As I left the taxi, I heard the driver mutter in heavily accented English, "Why anyone would want to spend the night here..."

I chuckled at his question as I strode towards the forest ranger that had met me there. The driver's remark was not unexpected, for he did not have the mind of a writer. Yes, spending the night in the Black Forest would seem like madness to most people, but for a horror novelist, it was heaven on earth.

I approached the ranger. In broken English he told me that he had received my note requesting to camp in the heart of the forest.

"And?' I asked impatiently.

"Sir, Black Forest is very large. Easy to get lost in it. Can be dangerous. Wolves live in heart of forest, and some animals...

I had already started at a run down the path into the forest.

3

My next book is going to be a masterpiece.

The Black Forest at night is exhilaratingly terrifying. How do I describe it? It doesn't feel haunted, per say, it feels... unsafe. I suppose it is the feeling of the unseen all around me. In my head, every hole in the ground is a gate to hell, every root a gargantuan snake, each noise a shriek, a hiss, a howl.

I love it.

Already, thoughts of stumbling through the forest with a faceless blood-drinker on my heels fill my brain. After ten minutes of walking, I found a spot where the trees opened out on a large ledge overlooking a steep twenty-foot drop. This is where I set up camp, and this is where I am writing in this diary now as I eat dinner. I've had a bit of sausage, but I'm not hungry. All I can think of is my book.

The Black Forest is exactly what I have been looking for. It provides BUCKETS of new material for writing horror. Now it is eleven o' clock, and I have a visual idea of the novel. Not entirely formulated, but it is one of my better plotlines.

But now my eyes grow heavy as thoughts of vampires and the undead crowd my mind...

4

My handwriting may be shaky.
Sorry. I'm bandaging my neck as I
write this. And my vision is blurry. And
it feels like someone beat the shit out
of my throat.

Let me try to explain.

I awoke on the hard, cold forest
floor feeling under-slept and unclean.
My mouth tasted like dirt. Pulling
myself up on one elbow, my watch told
me that it was two in the morning.

Ugh.

By this time my back had really
started to ache. I didn't care. I had
formulated the beginning of my book,
all that needed to be done now was to

write it down. I reached into my bag to retrieve a pen and paper, but instead I grabbed my flashlight as I heard a rustling noise in the trees above my head. Only one thought was going through my head now: *wolves don't climb trees.*

I traced the flashlight's beam along the tree line, illuminating leaves and bare branches. A chill ran down my back, and I shivered. For the first time, I truly began to experience true and utter fear. Whatever was in the trees was not showing itself.

"Hello?" I called, cursing how high-pitched my voice sounded as it reverberated in the clearing. I turned the flashlight upwards, and the beam of light fell across a thick branch, bent slightly by the weight of a man perched on its edge like a frog.

I have heard that once you see a person, you never truly forget him. I will never, no, can never forget this man. He wore all black, blending into the darkness perfectly, giving his pale head and hands the appearance of floating in the air. His shirt and pants were in tatters. His skin was chalk white, like every drop of color had been drained from his body and placed in his eyes.

My god, his eyes. They were a glittering crimson, not like blood, but like hardened magma waiting to erupt. Below a hooked nose shone his teeth, but they were not like teeth that I had ever seen. The upper canines were sharpened to razor points, and saliva dripped endlessly from his open maw.

For what seemed like an eternity, we just stared at each other. I felt small and helpless under his cruel gaze, like a bird caught between the claws of a cat. Every nerve in my body was screaming at me to run, to get as far from this inhuman being as fast as I could. But I felt rooted to the spot, captivated by the hypnotic hatred in his eyes.

And then he pitched forward, like a marionette doll whose strings had been cut, falling at impossible speed straight at me. The spell that had bound me broke, and I stumbled out of the way as he landed soundlessly, abnormally long nails raking the air in front of me. My tired mind was conjuring up all sorts of ways this could be a dream, a nightmare, a hallucination, anything but reality, and then a blur of teeth sped past me to my neck.

The most horrid pain exploded in my throat, like my windpipe was being slowly clawed out. I sunk to the ground as the pain began to build. My assailant grabbed my shoulders so I could not pull away, and I felt warm blood seep through my shirt as he let out an angry snarl and sunk his teeth into my neck again, with incredible precision, into the same spot as before. With a howl of pain, I wrenched myself away. I was aware of muttering, "Please no god no please god no no no." I repeated it over and over dully as I crawled away from the horrid creature (I refuse to call him a man, there is no way on earth he was human). He let me move away, once again studying my movements. I was the prey, and he was the hunter, patiently waiting for the chance to deliver the killing blow.

For the first time, I was aware of my flashlight, still clenched tightly in my hand. As the monstrosity came bearing down on me again, his teeth bared, I swung the heavy metal device up into his face. A shower of blood sprayed me, followed by a sickening crunch. Enraged, he lunged for me, emitting a spitting, hissing noise like an angry snake, blood flying in red ropes from his mouth. Total fear and adrenaline gripped me and I leapt to the side as he flew past, his hands outstretched to grab me.

What I knew was that the creature was trying to kill me. What I had *forgotten* was the twenty-foot drop off where I had been camping. He careened headfirst over the side of the cliff, followed by a bloodcurdling shriek, a snap, and then silence.

...

For a while, I just lay there, letting the oppressive silence pound into my ears. Then, mustering up my courage, I crawled to the edge of the cliff and looked down.

My attacker's body lay in a crumpled heap at the bottom. In the light of the moon, I beheld his grisly fate. A broken tree branch, jutting up from the ground at the bottom of the cliff, had gone clean through his chest. His shattered ribs stuck out like twigs from the fatal wound. The ground all around him was dark with blood.

Ignoring the pain in my neck and every instinct telling me not to, I jumped over the cliff, using the side of it as a brake to slow my fall. My shoes kicked up dust and made a rough scraping noise along the side of the rock face until I reached the bottom. Cautiously, I approached the corpse in front of me.

No pulse. No breath. No sign that he was alive. I leaned in to get a closer look at his face, and his scarlet eyes flew open. Quick as lightning, a white hand shot out and wrapped itself around my throat. He stared at me, but all hatred and anger had left his eyes. Instead, there was... sadness? Relief? I couldn't tell. His eyes drifted to the bite on my neck, and his eyes filled with tears. All he said, in a raspy, cracked, barely audible whisper, was, "You... it continues with you. I'm so sorry..."

His voice faded. His hand went slack, and he fell back on the ground, his horrid teeth shining in the moonlight, scarlet with my own blood.

5

As soon as the sun came up, I notified the ranger and got the hell out of the forest. We had both agreed that the incident would never be spoken of, as attempted murder was not something to advertise about a place, and, despite my horrifying experience, I could not bear to see such an outstanding outlet of ideas be shut down. The ranger had, however, muttered under his breath as I got into the taxi that morning, "I warned you."

Breakfast at the airport consisted of a dry morning roll, which I ate without really tasting it. The pain in my neck had reduced to a dull throb,

and I was able to put it out of my
thoughts as I boarded the plane. It
returned, however, about halfway
through the flight. I awoke from a nap
to the low thrum of the engines, and I
rubbed the sleep out of my eyes.

For a few seconds, I thought it
was turbulence that had awoken me.
Then again, I never slept well on
planes, even in first class. This was
because people tended to stare at the
famous author while I tried to sleep,
making dozing impossible.

But that was not what had woken
me up this time. As my eyes grew heavy
again, I suddenly felt a prickly, faint
pain in my neck. I reached back to my
throat and picked at the spot with my
index finger.

My first huge mistake.

An EXPLOSION of pain met my touch. Nothing I had ever experienced could amount to this. I keeled over in my seat, nausea racking me, trying desperately not to scream. My knuckles were white on the armrests of my chair, and my hands were trembling uncontrollably as I waited, no, prayed, for the fit of agony to pass.

And pass it did. Unbuckling my seatbelt, I stumbled to the bathroom, finally earning myself some very strange looks from the other passengers.

I locked the door to the small cubicle and faced the smudged mirror. My tired, unshaven face stared back. I was alarmed at how pale my reflection looked, but that had to be a trick of the dim bathroom light. And surely, I could blame the tint of scarlet I noticed in my eyes on lack of sleep as I stared into the mirror. Even so, I was unsettled.

Tilting my neck upwards, I observed the bite on my neck. It was amazing that something so small could cause so much pain. Two miniscule pinpricks stood out on my skin, slightly irritated and red around their edges. I did not dare touch them again, lest I suffer as I had in my seat.

Sleep eluded me for the rest of the time I was on the plane. I occupied myself with writing my book, but I had not gotten very far into it before I was afflicted with the worst sickness any writer can come down with- writer's block. There is nothing, and I mean *nothing* more annoying or frustrating to a professional writer than rolling along with your story, everything going perfectly, and then having it come to a crashing halt. There is no medication, no way to treat it. All one can do is wait for it to pass.

As I sat there with my computer sitting in my lap, I thought to pull out my diary. After writing the events of the morning, my thoughts turned to Maria back home in Manhattan. Ah, Miss Bennet, how I have missed your touch, your voice, your writing. Maria

Bennet, light of my life, I am coming home.

6

As soon as my transfer plane landed, I hailed a cab, ran up to my apartment, and passed out on my sofa. Apologies. This is why I didn't write in my diary yesterday. I slept for a full day; I felt completely drained of energy. I didn't even take my shoes off before letting sleep overtake me. Even the dull pain of my neck could not stop my slumber. For the first time, I found that sleeping during the day proved easy for me to do.

When I awoke, my mouth tasted like bad breath and spit, and there was a gnawing hole of hunger in my stomach. I found that someone had thrown a blanket over me. Sitting up, I noticed a faint glow coming from my previously dark kitchen. Throwing the blanket off of me, I crept into the kitchen.

If anyone but Maria Bennet had been sitting in my kitchen reading a book, I would have freaked out. However, my girlfriend and I entered and left each other's apartments as we pleased. We trusted each other greatly.

My footfalls were silent on the wooden floor as I crept up behind her. Putting my lips to Maria's ear, I said in a deep but loud voice, "Boo."

Maria jumped clean out of the chair. "James!" she exclaimed in a subtle New York accent, the slight quaver in her voice betraying the fear she had felt. Giving me an annoyed punch on the shoulder, she said, "You know I hate it when you do that."

For the first time in days, I laughed. I am thirty-five, one year Maria's senior. We met at a writer's convention in upstate New York, when I was still relatively new to the writing world. She asked to read one of the books I had with me, and I had read one of hers. Soon, we had started chatting, went out and got a drink, and our relationship went from there. Maria shares my passion for writing and reading, traits that I value in people. Unlike me, however, her specialty was mystery thrillers. Her hair is of the darkest raven black, and her hazel green eyes stand out beautifully on her tanned face.

After a kiss hello, she settled back in her chair and passed me the laptop. "What do you think?" I said as I closed the screen. Maria knit her eyebrows, which is what she did when she was thinking.

"Overall, to be honest, it could use some work," she said. "You jump into the plot too quickly. Build it up. I want to get to know the hero a bit more. What's his background? And where did you get the idea of 'The Black Forest?'"

I sighed. "It's a very long story."

For ten minutes, I relayed my experiences in the Black Forest back to Maria (I must remember that for the title of my book. *An Experience in the Black Forest*. Yes, that roles off the tongue nicely). I did not, however, mention the attack. Why worry her? She listened intently to the rest of it the whole time.

After I finished the story, I arose and crossed to the fridge, from which I fished out two cold beers. I didn't normally drink the stuff, except on special occasions. I set one of them down in front of Maria, and for a while we just sat there in the dim light, sipping our drinks.

Then, from across the table I caught Maria's eye as she was in mid-sip. Her lips were pursed around the edge of the bottle like she was puckering up to kiss it, and for some reason I thought that was hilarious. I burst out laughing, and Maria, when she realized why, joined in. For reasons unknown, we couldn't stop laughing.

Finally, Maria, still chortling, got up to retrieve a tissue to wipe her eyes. I settled back in my chair and smiled. No moments in my life, not even when I was writing, could amount to the times I spent with Maria. For a few minutes, my mind had even been completely taken off of my neck.

That was until Maria returned, still smiling contentedly. She sat down again and threw her arms around me. She whispered in my ear, her breath warm on my face, "I'm glad you're back."

She turned in her seat and brought her mouth to mine. I welcomed her ensuing kisses with my own, until her arms came to lay on my neck.

When you experience unmatched, unyielding pain, your vision goes red. That was what happened when Maria's arms rested on my bite wound. A wave of pain, even worse than the one on the plane, hit me with the force of a speeding train. Every nerve in my neck seemed to be on fire. I emitted a guttural scream, and Maria jumped back, alarmed.

"James, what happened? What did I do?" she asked, bewildered. I couldn't reply. My neck felt like acid was searing it away. With my eyes

scrunched tight, I muttered, "My neck."
Maria tilted my chin back with her
hand and stared at the wound. I heard
her gasp sharply.

"My god. I didn't notice that
when you came in..."

"What is it?" I managed to ask.
The pain was fading again, but it still
throbbed slightly. My head pounded as
Maria helped me stand up and led me
to the bathroom. Flicking on the light,
I stared at my neck in the mirror.

The wound had puffed up, red
and swollen. Sickly yellow liquid ran
down the side of it, and the veins
around the bite had swelled up, the
color of puke. It looked like the bite
would burst any minute, and it
appeared to me, like it was *pulsing*.

Like it was alive.

I held in a gag. The thought of a living, growing wound repulsed me, but at least the pain had passed. Coming out of the bathroom, I managed a shaky smile for Maria. Her eyes still radiated concern, but I tried to wave it aside. "I'll get it looked at this week. It's probably just an infected cut I got in the forest."

Lying to Maria was not an easy thing to do, partly because she was not one to be fooled easily. She did not say anymore on the matter, however, so perhaps she believed me. My neck bothered me no more that night, though for some reason I could not fall asleep that night. Long after Maria and I retired to bed, I tossed and

turned, unable to keep my eyes closed.
It was as if my body had forgotten
how to sleep. I finally achieved
slumber as the sun began to rise over
New York City.

7

I am going to talk about teeth.

Hear me out. In all my years, I have had only four cavities, a little root canal treatment, and my wisdom teeth pulled. My teeth are clean. I have had very few tooth problems. Until today.

The day after I got back, all I did was sleep. I'm serious. I didn't even wake up to eat or use the bathroom. By the time I awoke this morning, it was one in the afternoon, and the sun was high in the sky. I felt under-slept and tired, and I was about to turn over and have another few hours of rest when I felt something odd.

An aching pain in my mouth. Not bad, just noticeable enough that it hurt. Curious, I rubbed my jaw and got out of bed. I padded over to the bathroom, my footfalls making faint slapping noises on the tile floor. Bleary-eyed, I faced the mirror and opened my mouth.

The gums above my top canine teeth were grotesquely swollen and red, much like my neck, I realized with a jolt. What if the two were related? My gaze traveled to my teeth. At first I couldn't see anything wrong with them. They looked just as they always had, with a touch of white plaque on the edges. But as I leaned in closer to the mirror, I noticed something.

My canine teeth had elongated. Not very far, but the tips had thinned and sharpened into fine points. I rubbed my eyes to clear them. Perhaps I was imagining that. No, my fanglike canines still pointed out at me from my mouth. I reached out, pinched one between my fingers, and gave it a little nudge. Nothing happened. The tooth seemed rooted into my gums like all of my others. The gum around the tooth, however, turned a shade of dark, ugly red.

I thought back to the Black Forest, where my attacker had used his long, sharp teeth to pierce my neck, which had been bothering me ever since then. His fangs were almost identical to the ones in my mouth. I shuddered. The thought of transforming into my adversary was ghastly to think about. *I'm not like him*, I reminded myself as I started to shave. *I'm not a murderous monster.*

I spent the morning at my kitchen table, eating cereal I hardly tasted while I read and wrote. I have found that when one is afflicted with writer's block, reading is the best remedy. From the morning into the late afternoon, I read and highlighted the pages of books like *Dracula*, *Interview with the Vampire*, and *Varney the Vampire*, or *The Feast of Blood*.

The authors had very different styles of writing horror. Stoker wanted to scare his readers with the possibility that Dracula could overrun the world with vampirism, while Anne Rice chose a more horrific approach, better suited for the modern age. I disliked James Malcom Ryder's *Varney the Vampire*, however, as getting through the author's 812 pages of gothic horror could be challenging.

However, I could not deny in any of the books I read that morning the author's genius of character. Vampires came in so many shapes and sizes, from giant bats to suave, sensual creatures of the night. I even skimmed back through *Twilight* to read more about Edward's character (I had a lot of time on my hands).

After getting halfway through *Varney the Vampire*, I set the thick volume down on the table and looked at my watch. Four thirty. More than enough time to get ready for a night to remember.

I am about to take Maria out on a date to a new, fancy restaurant in the Lower East Side, followed by a quiet stroll along Manhattan's dark streets. As I buttoned up my white dress shirt, feeling its crisp texture on my skin, my fingers brushed up against my neck, but only a faint twinge met my touch. I smiled.

Everything was going to go right tonight.

I could feel it in my blood.

Of all the horrific and unexplained experiences of the past few days, I think tonight tops them all.

I don't mean the DATE, of course. The beginning of it was lovely. I picked up Maria at her apartment, and we took a cab to the restaurant. The setting sun cast an orange light over the darkening street as Maria and I arrived at the restaurant. Slow Jazz music floated out from behind its doors, and the aromas of various foods wafted from the kitchen. A waiter sat us at a free table outside, and for a while Maria and I just sat and talked.

"So when do you plan to finish your book?" Maria asked as she took a small sip of red wine. Like me, Maria drank rarely. When she wrote, she would sometimes drink to clear her head. I disapproved of this way of writing, but for her it was effective; Maria sold many books.

"Honestly, I'm not entirely sure," I replied. "Personally, I think my experience in the Black Forest scared me too much to write my good ideas down."

Maria's eyes narrowed with suspicion. "You've avoided the subject until now. What exactly happened in that forest? You haven't been the same since you got back."

"Er..." I realized too late that I had given something away. Maria was anything but stupid, and it wasn't taking her long to put two and two together.

Maria leaned in closer and lowered her voice. "It's that mark on your neck, isn't it?" she said. "You were practically dying when I touched it yesterday."

I sighed and pulled back the collar of my shirt. Obviously, Maria and I would not be having pleasant conversation tonight. I felt the cool night air blow against my neck, and Maria said, "Huh."

"What is it?" I asked. For a few seconds I was worried that the bite had grown worse, but Maria's tone indicated mild surprise, not alarm.

"It shrunk," she said simply, and she pulled out her hand mirror from her purse and moved it in front of my throat. So it had. The marks seemed to have deflated. They were still red-rimmed around their edges, but they had stopped leaking that yellow puss.

"I don't understand this," I said. "It was absolutely *grotesque* just last night. How can it have healed overnight?"

A sudden shadow of fear passed over Maria's face. "You know, I read about this happening once. I was at the library with a lot of time on my hands, and I found this old manuscript in the archives."

I leaned forward. Books were something I could relate to. "What was it about? Could this all just be a medical malady?" I felt bad about lying to her. A sickness hadn't been what had attacked me in the forest. I presumed I would have to keep searching for explanations to my plight.

But Maria surprised me by saying, "No, the manuscript told the story of a chain of murders in Serbia, due to what was believed to be a freshly dead man that returned from the grave to drink the blood of the people in his village."

"A vampire," I said. For some reason, the word sent a shiver down my spine. It had never occurred to me that I had been attacked by a vampire, but it would make sense in Wallachia, especially since my attacker had gone for my neck. However, I was skeptical to believe it. Vampires did not exist on earth. They were a work of fiction. I should know.

Maria continued, "The man was a soldier named Arnold Paole. After a war he returned home, claiming to have been attacked by a vampire while in the service. A few days later, Paole was crushed to death by a wagon."

"Ouch."

"A few weeks later, reports of Paole roaming the land around the town's cemetery came up. Along with these sightings came a terrible sickness, in which the afflicted person lost blood until they paled and died in agony. Finally, the townspeople had had enough. Storming the graveyard, they unearthed Paole's body. The corpse should have been decaying; instead he was rosy-cheeked, healthy, and... filled to the brim with the blood of his victims.

She shuddered. "Sorry. The text kind of goes into detail. Anyway, the townspeople sprinkled garlic around his tomb, the initial way to repel a vampire, then they stabbed a wooden stake through his heart. The corpse decomposed, and they sealed the tomb shut so he couldn't get out."

Maria finished her story and sat back in her chair. Her eyes bore into me as she said, "I'll ask again, James. *What happened in that forest?*"

I finally told her about the attack. Maria just sat there, drinking in the impossible story coming from my lips. I did not go into the grim details of my misadventure, only that my assailant had accidentally brought about his own demise when he attacked me. As I spoke, my neck began to throb for the first time that night.

Like it was angry.

I was interrupted by the arrival of our food. The delicious smell of filet mignon wafted to my nose as the waiter set it down in front of me. Maria had ordered lobster, which also smelled fragrant. My mouth watering in anticipation, I traced my tongue along the sharp ridges of my canine teeth, waiting to sink them into the succulent steak (I write better when I imagine food).

Was I just so hungry I just imagined what happened next? Was the talk of vampires and blood too much for me? As the waiter turned to leave, his shape shimmered like a reflection in water before my eyes. Maria had started her lobster like nothing was happening, but I watched, transfixed, as the waiter's form swam once more, and then something truly unexplainably horrific occurred.

The waiter's skin and clothes shimmered once more and... liquefied. Underneath, I watched in silent horror and fascination as his bones came into focus. His skull glowed an eerie green, like some kind of living x-ray. As his organs solidified, glowing a neon orange color, a low, deep, resounding noise began to beat in my ears like a large drum. It was like all the blood had rushed to my head in three seconds.

Not my blood, I realized as I felt bile rise in my throat, his.

The man's pulsing, crimson, quivering heart sat in his chest, and the blue veins leading into it were tight with the fresh blood that pounded in my ears. All thoughts of my dinner vanished; I was overtaken by a stabbing, senseless hunger, an irresistible urge to reach out and rip the man's beating heart from his chest, to hear his agonized scream, to taste the warm, red blood on my tongue...

I extended my hands like a blind man and lunged.

My eyes flew open. The only blood I could taste in my mouth was my own, as I had landed face-first on the hard, stone floor of the restaurant. The low murmur of the people seated around me mixed with the dying noise of the blood in my ears. The waiter, his skin no longer shimmering, stood off to the side, his body taut with surprise.

I felt a hand on my shoulder, and I turned to see Maria, who helped me back into my seat. The waiter, getting over his initial surprise, cautiously approached the table with a wet cloth. I pressed it to my mouth to stem the flow of blood.

Maria waited until our waiter left, then turned back to me. Her eyes were filled with confusion, surprise, and anger. And Maria Bennet was not someone you wanted angry at you. She hissed in a furious whisper, "What the hell was that about? *You jumped the waiter.*"

A cold feeling blossomed in the pit of my stomach. "Excuse me?"

She pointed at the bloodstain on the stone pavement. "One moment, everything is fine, you're about to dig into your meal, fork and knife in hand, the next, you positively *leap* out of your chair to try to attack our waiter! You tripped and ended up on the ground with blood pouring from your mouth. What insanity compelled you to do that?"

Maria seemed to realize that I didn't know either what had happened. She leaned over and took my hands in hers. "Go to the doctor this week. I want you to be okay. Just please, make sure you're fine."

My face felt hot with shame. I had completely lost my appetite. For the first time that night, my neck bite began to hurt, mixing with the growing pain of my fangs.

What the hell is happening to me?

9

I dropped Maria back at her apartment later that night. I had insisted that I only needed a bit of fresh air, but I doubt she believed me after such talk of vampires. We left the restaurant and walked back to her apartment building.

A beautiful moon was high in the cloudless sky, shrouded only by the smoke wafting from surrounding buildings. She opened the door of the building, then stopped. She turned to me, and her face was almost completely shrouded in the darkness in the night. She looked like a bride dressed in the folds of the night, with a black veil of darkness laid over her face.

"James," she said, her voice echoing slightly in the stairwell. She paused again, and I knew she was searching for words to say. Evidently she could not find any, for after a quick kiss goodnight, she closed the door.

...

New York never slept. Even at midnight, when the cab dropped me at my apartment, I could hear the roar of cars and could see the flashing of bright lights from deep inside the city. I yawned as I entered the apartment. I was exhausted, but I would not sleep on this cursed night. Tonight was a night of research.

I quietly closed the door to my apartment and didn't bother to turn on the lights. The heavy, black silence was more soothing to me than lights and noise, but I flipped open the screen to my laptop anyway, letting its white glow fill the space. Clicking on the Safari icon, I typed in, 'Vampirism.'

The page flooded with articles and stories. Rubbing the exhaustion out of my eyes, I began to scroll down the page. I noticed the story of Arnold Paole among the articles as I searched. I finally found an article titled *Signs of Vampirism*, and I opened it up. A bulleted list appeared on the screen, and I began to read.

10

Vampirism

For centuries, vampires have been the stuff of legend in Eastern European cities and towns. Tales of the dead reanimated as blood sucking ghosts, preying on their former loved ones, have worked their way into American culture as well, through books and movies. Vampires, however, are sometimes thought to be more than just a myth. Accounts of vampire attacks and encounters helped to create this list of their characteristics and physical traits.

- Vampires have extremely pale skin, as they never go into sunlight
- Their upper canines are as sharp as needles, used for penetrating the jugular vein of their victims. This is their most defining trait.

Fang sizes can vary, depending on the size of the vampire's teeth when he was human

- A vampire's eye color changes depending on their mood, but their original eye color is a deep blood-red
- Vampires possess immense strength, sometimes being able to lift the weight of ten men
- Vampires possess the power of Hypnotism
- Vampires do not appear in mirrors. As the victim begins to transform, his reflection will begin to fade in mirrors
- In the days leading up to the final transformation, the victim will lose his appetite for food, as it has been replaced by an insatiable lust for fresh human blood

- Vampires have the ability to change their shape, turning into fog or an assortment of animals, like bats, wolves, and owls. They can also morph into mist or smoke, to get into a victim's room

Ways of Becoming a Vampire

Vampires pass down their eternal curse to their victims in multiple ways. Sometimes, humans may even unintentionally bring the curse of vampirism upon themselves. The virus spreads faster in a smaller community, as the vampire has fewer victims to infect.

- DIRECT WAY: The vampire will normally enter a victim's house in smoke form, as he cannot enter a house in solid form without being invited first. Once inside, he selects a victim to infect, makes an incision along his or her jugular with his canine teeth, and drinks the flowing blood

- VAMPIRE ATTACK: If a vampire directly attacks its victim, it starts the transformation, even if the victim does not come into contact with the vampire again

- DRINKING A VAMPIRE'S BLOOD: If a vampire convinces his victim to approach him at night, he then uses his hypnotic gaze to get the victim to drink his own blood from a vein in his chest. This speeds up the human's transformation and bonds the vampire to his victim for life

- SUICIDE: If a human, infected already or not, commits suicide, he or she is reanimated as a vampire

- NOTE: If a vampire is not fully transformed, the bite does not pass down the curse to the victim

Ways of killing a vampire

While vampires possess immense strength and magic, they can be killed. Over the centuries, vampire hunters have discovered multiple ways to end the misery of the undead.

- BLOOD LOSS: If a vampire has not had blood for some time, he will lose his healthy appearance, taking on a decrepit, older form. Eventually, the vampire will go into a sort of hibernation, until fresh blood revives him again
- WOODEN STAKES: According to myth, a wooden stake will kill a vampire when it is stabbed through his heart. This may or may not be accurate, but a wooden stake *will*

pin a vampire to his coffin, preventing him from leaving

- SUNLIGHT: A fully transformed vampire's reaction to sunlight is horrid and fatal. It will either crumble into ashes, take on a decomposing, petrified appearance, or simply explode, showering the blood of its past victims everywhere like a mosquito

- BULLETS: Vampires are not werewolves. Any type of bullet will kill them, although it will take many to bring a vampire down. Knives, however, do not affect them

- CRUCIFIXES: When a vampire comes into physical contact with a holy crucifix, his skin will blister and smoke where the cross touches him, and if one is placed in a vampire's tomb, it will be difficult for him to leave it

- FINAL NOTE: Do not jump to conclusions if you suspect someone of being a vampire. Even though vampires are widely believed to be works of fiction, one should not engage someone suspected of vampirism in combat.

I sat back from the computer screen, my eyes fuzzy from staring at it for so long.

Works of fiction.

Was it a "work of fiction" that almost murdered me in the Black Forest? Was it a "work of fiction" that I *seemed to be transforming into?*

I caught myself. No. There was no such thing as vampires. They were the creation of writers like me, bent on scaring the world with our genius. They were a tool for fear, just another monster I could write about.

Right?

From an early age, we are taught to scoff at the idea of monsters. They are figments of the imagination, unreal beings that should be both revered and reviled. They are immortalized in books, but the key reason of why monsters are the tool of authors around the world is because *they do not exist*.

The goal of a horror writer is to explain the unexplained to his readers. To scare them, yes, but to also assure them that whatever horrific or unnatural happenings in their books are *not true*. To have that proved untrue... to believe that vampires walk among the living... it goes against every rational thought.

And yet...

I am not a superstitious man. Even if I witness something unnatural occur with my own eyes, I need to be totally convinced that I saw it. Though I make a career writing about it, I do not believe in the supernatural. But whatever was happening to me was *not* natural. And I needed to know what it was.

Turning back to my laptop, I scrolled down the list until I found the author's name. Dr. George Morton, *specialist in the field of vampirism.*

It looked like I was going to the doctor's after all.

11

9917, Carrey St.

The address was printed on a copper plaque nailed to the door of George Morton's townhouse. I had to take MetroNorth to get to the Rye suburb, where he resided. Now, standing in front of his house, I was having second thoughts. His home looked like a grease smudge in the midst of the prim, white houses clumped next to it. The faded black wood was covered with a chipped black paint, and a crooked chimney snaked into the smoky sky. The house's windows were open, but no movement came from behind them.

As I walked up the driveway, however, I must admit that I had expected far worse, no matter how eerie this house looked. When I thought *vampire expert*, I had imagined an overflowing garden of garlic, a crucifix on the front door, and maybe a sign or two that said *stakes 4 life*.

Still, I couldn't help shivering slightly as I mounted the porch steps. The house just looked so... dead, completely devoid of color. But maybe that was what Morton had gone for, an undead house blended in among the living ones. I came to the dark oak door and took the knocker in my hand. It was shaped like a bat.

I let it fall against the door, sending a low *crack* through the thick wood. I heard muffled footsteps coming towards me, and then the door opened to reveal a striking man of about fifty years, with a trimmed greying beard and icy blue eyes that had an uncountable number of crinkles around their edges. He was dressed in a black traveler's suit that gave the appearance that he was about to leave the house in a hurry.

Altogether, the look was slightly intimidating. He surveyed me in silence for a time, and then I said, rather timidly, "Are you George Morton?"

"That I am," he replied in a deep voice. "What do you need, sir?" it struck me that I *could* see this man striding through a cemetery at night with a wooden dagger clenched in his hand. Which brought me back to why I had come here.

But I didn't know how to say it. Have you ever found it impossible to word something correctly, either when speaking or writing? I had that problem here as I was faced by this imposing man. Could I just say, *yes, I believe I am transforming into a vampire, could you confirm it before you put a stake through my heart? Yes,* that would go down nicely.

Finally, I knew what to say. "I have a problem that falls into your area of expertise," I said, and tilted my head back to reveal the bite on my neck. The next thing I knew, I was being whisked into the house and sat down in a dark red velvet armchair.

Morton sat across from me, pulled out a notepad and pencil, and began to pepper me with questions.

"Name?"

"J-James Henry Henning."

"Age?"

I felt like I was in some kind of interrogation. "Thirty-five."

"Day of bite?"

That question resounded in my ears like the waiter's blood. I thought back to when I wrote in my diary about the attack and the date came into my head.

"The 24th of September."

"Symptoms since bite?"

"Uh... dizziness, extreme pain in my neck, tooth growth, pallor, and strange hallucinations."

Morton scribbled it all down, put down the pad of paper, and extended his hand.

"Apologies for the brisk welcome. I'm George Morton, expert in vampire myths, legends, and lore. Unfortunately, I always need to do that when someone with this kind of case visits me. It helps me evaluate their progress later on."

I shook his hand firmly, and then I finally got the chance to look around the room we were in. Just like my apartment, the walls were stacked with books, but they were *all* of the vampire genre. I hadn't realized there were this many vampire novels in the world, and I felt a stab of disappointment when I remembered

that I had not yet completed mine.
Soon, though, I hoped to see my novel
on that shelf, with *New York Times*
bestselling author printed on the front
in bold letters...

Sorry. Going off topic again. I
turned back to Morton, but he had
gotten up and was standing at the
other side of the room, sorting through
a second bookshelf. Still turned away
from me, he said, "You're that author
that always brags about traveling for
ideas for his books, right?"

A surge of annoyance passed over
me. "I don't *brag* about it!" I said
indignantly. Who did this high and
mighty doctor think he was, saying that
I bragged about my work?

"Brag, talk about it, publicize it worldwide, doesn't make much difference," he said as he pulled a thick volume from the shelf. Turning back to me, he muttered, almost too himself, "I wondered when you'd travel to Romania. He set down the book on the table between us.

"How did you"- I began, but he waved the question away. "Where else would you go to write a story about vampires? Where vampires reside most, of course. Now, down to business."

He flipped through the book until he came to a page titled *The Vampyre*. The same list I had seen online was printed in gothic speech on the page. "Can you describe the hallucinations you suffered, Mr. Henning?" Morton asked, picking up the book, marking his page, and thumbing through it again.

"Well, that morning I had woken up to find that my teeth had elongated to fine points. I didn't think much of it until I took my girlfriend out to dinner, and when the food arrived, I"-

"Saw through your waiter, seeing the blood inside of him," the doctor finished. I stared at him, amazed. A small smile played across his lips. "I am a vampire specialist, Mr. Henning. I know more than I let on. And I take my work very seriously."

He stood from his chair and beckoned for me to follow him. Still slightly surprised, I did. We walked through the house, into a long gallery of paintings, all of them depicting acts of vampirism. We stopped at a painting depicting a pale, thin man with dark crimson stains on his chin, pursuing a beautiful woman.

As I inspected the work, I noticed that the artist had drawn the woman's veins and bones darker and more defined under her skin, like they were just below the surface, waiting to jump out of her. The painting's detail was amazing, and I took in the rich hues the artist had painted in the dark landscape. The woman was depicted running from the pale man, and he seemed to be reaching out to her, if it was in a pleading gesture or an attacking one, I was not sure. At the bottom of the painting, the artist had written the name of his work.

Der Blutsauger.

Just two simple words, but once again, I felt a shiver run down my spine as I read them. "That's German," I said pointing at the title of the painting.

"Yes," Said Morton, also staring at the painting. "This was made in the late sixteenth century, around the time that vampire hysteria was rising in Europe. At that time, people were more superstitious and uneducated about vampire lore, so nights were lived in fear in eastern European villages. No one came out of their houses at night.

"Even though the vampire was mainly the subject of stories told to entertain and frighten, people took the myth very seriously. Any traces of vampirism were enough for a mob of superstitious villagers to storm a nearby cemetery in search of the infection. Over the years, the vampire's powers and characteristics became more evident, and soon enough, the legend traveled to the new world, where it resides today."

Morton stopped talking. I stared in bewilderment at him. "But vampires are just a harmless myth! A story to be told around campfires! Those that take it seriously must not be right in the head..."

The doctor shook his head. He rubbed his temples in a stressed manner, then gestured back to the painting. "The artist wasn't insane. Vampires are as real as you or me, much more real than any other presumably fictitious creature. And you, my unfortunate man," he pointed at me, as if convicting me of some heinous crime, "You have been infected with the curse of vampirism."

12

I wanted to believe he was joking. Every rational thought told me that Dr. George Morton was as batty as the vampires he studied. I could have walked out of his dead house right then and there and let events play out.

But I didn't. Somehow, by some crazy stretch of truth, the doctor's words actually made sense. That was what scared me. The broken pieces of the puzzle of what had happened to me seemed to be fitting together. And as they did so, my neck began to ache.

I followed George out of the gallery, hot on his heels. "Whoa, whoa, back up, Morton. You can't just say something like that and not expect me to have"-

Morton turned abruptly, and I almost ran into him. This time, his face was annoyed behind his grey beard. "You think this is some kind of *joke?* Some subject for a crackpot novel? A *curable* malady? You have no idea what you have unleashed when you foolishly trekked in Romania. A black hole of death itself has opened inside of you," he poked my chest with his finger, "And it will never close, just like the bite on your neck."

I fell back. Morton's gaze softened slightly and he said, "I'm sorry. I cannot cure you. You have been tainted with the bite of a vampire. His saliva now runs through your veins, infecting your body as we speak. But I can make sure that no one you love is at risk."

My hopes rose. It had never crossed my mind that I could hurt Maria, or the other people in my apartment. "Could you? I would pay any price..."

The doctor waved my offer aside. "There is no price for saving New York city from a fate worse than death. Just do as I say, and we may even be able to slow your transformation. I take it you viewed my website?"

I nodded. "Well, if you start developing any other symptoms or features that I listed, come back here at once. Even the smallest sign of progression can mean that you are completely transformed. In the meantime, stay away from rare meats and hospitals. Stay out of the sunlight when possible."

I looked up. "Hospitals? Rare meats?" I asked, confused.

"The mere sight of blood could drive you into a killing frenzy, quickening the transformation," explained the doctor distractedly, crossing the room to a shelf and pulling out a long syringe. "Hold out your arm."

The mild sting as the needle entered my vein made me wince. I watched as my own blood moved slowly up the tube. Morton pulled the needle out, and flicked it. The blood sloshed around inside. I felt mildly queasy as I watched him deposit the blood into a glass vial, which he sealed with a rubber stopper. Morton turned back to me.

"I'm going to take a closer look at your blood. Depending on how much it's mutated, we can figure out how close you are to finishing the transformation. Until then, I must bid you goodbye."

He led me to the door, but as I opened it, he gripped my arm tightly. "Remember what I said, Mr. Henning. You are a danger to the world around you. Tread with caution. If any other transformations take place, notify me only. If anyone asks where you were today, tell them you had a doctor's appointment. And do not, under any circumstances, come into contact with human blood."

With that, I stepped out of 9917 and into the cold, crisp, grey autumn day, the few trees that were lining the sidewalk reaching out to me like dead fingers.

13

My apologies for not writing in this diary for a while. Nothing particularly *freaky* occurred in the past week. Until today, when the transformation began to take a turn for the worst.

I have no idea what triggered it. For the past few days, I had done exactly what the doctor had said; I steered clear of hospitals. I had not eaten any rare meats. I even refrained from watching TV, lest I witness the sight of blood in some movie.

Distancing myself from Maria, however, was the hardest part. What was I supposed to tell her, *doctor's* order, I can't spend time with you because I might expose you to a horrid mythical curse. Sorry. She had called my apartment multiple times, but I had not picked up. Somehow, hearing her voice but not seeing her would have made it even more difficult.

On Friday, I was sitting in an armchair writing. I had almost finished my book, but it was not a work I was particularly proud of. My writing was not at its best when I had a familiar ache in my neck. The phone on the nightstand rang, showing Maria's number in glowing green letters. I waited for it to stop, then listened to the message she recorded.

"James, if you're there, please pick up. I don't know what happened at your appointment, but *please* don't push me away because of it. I want to be there for you, but I can't if you shut the door in my face. Love you. Bye."

I sat in the silence that followed, listening to the low ringtone of the phone. Finally, with a heavy heart, I deleted the message. There was no way I was going to see Maria, not until I got back the results from Morton. With a sigh, I sat back in my chair.

...

I finally decided that some fresh air would do me good. I had barely left the apartment all week, and though I was wary of the doctor's instructions, I decided that a quick stroll of no more than a few blocks couldn't hurt.

There is a good reason why they say *follow the doctor's orders.*

I stepped out of my apartment into the crisp autumn day. The cold weather had come early to New York this year, and the chill numbed my fingers as I began my walk. The sun was just beginning to dip behind the skyscrapers, throwing everything into an orange light. The wind blew through my hair and my shoes made low thumping sounds on the sidewalk with each step.

At dusk, especially during the fall, New York seemed quieter in a way. The smoky air seemed to dull the distant noises of cars and construction, pressing down like a blanket on the city. The colors seemed to dim around me, like an old fashioned black- and-white movie screen, making the grey in the buildings stand out against the cold sun. It was a good time to be alone with one's thoughts.

I wondered what George Morton was doing with my blood at that moment. Could he have already made a diagnosis from studying it? Part of me didn't want him to succeed. If he had scientific evidence that I was a vampire, then there was no chance of denying it. I wanted to hold onto the rational thoughts in my head, telling me that the dead could not live again, but I was finding it harder and harder to do so.

And then there was the nagging voice in the back of my head, saying over and over and over again.

What will Maria say?

Shut up. I don't even know if I even am one or not.

You still think she'll love you?

Of course!

You think she'll love you if you become a blood-sucking zombie?

...

See? Even you don't believe it.

What did I do to get stuck with you, brain?

Overall, I was most worried about hurting her. If I did something I regretted, I would never forgive myself. At the same time, distancing myself was hurting us both.

Finally, I made a decision. As I walked, I pulled out my cell-phone and dialed her number. Immediately, Maria's frantic voice came out on the other end.

"James, where the *hell* have you been? You haven't answered my calls, responded to my messages, and your landlord says he hasn't seen you for days! I've been worried sick!"

A pang of guilt blossomed in the pit of my stomach. "Listen," I said, and when I didn't hear an angry retort from the other end, I continued, "I went to a special kind of doctor. His name is George Morton and he specializes in vampirism."

Que her anger. Que the explanation.

"He took a sample of my blood to look at, to see if there's anything… supernaturally wrong with me. He's going to get back to me soon. Until then, he told me to limit all contact with blood and those close to me."

I waited for her to process the message. Finally, she spoke.

"Come to my apartment tomorrow night. I need to see you."

A shadow of doubt passed over me. "The doctor said"-

"To hell with what Morton said. He's not your girlfriend. I don't believe that isolating yourself solves anything. Tomorrow night. My place. Don't forget."

She hung up. I clicked my phone shut and continued walking. Now I was conflicted. Do what Morton said, or spend time with (and possibly endanger) Maria?

When your rational mind sides with the wrong decision, there's not much you can do.

I decided I would go to Maria's. Surely, I assured myself, *the transformation can't take total control in the course of a day.*

In the next second, something happened that did *not* drive that thought home. My head began to swim, and I felt dizzy. A coppery, metallic smell wafted past me, and then...

My vision began to shimmer. Peculiar crimson, glowing lines

manifested in my vison, travelling to my nose. I realized it was the peculiar scent I had picked up. And the scent, just like the transparent waiter, made me gut-wrenchingly hungry.

I began to run, following the smell. I heard a car's horn at the side of my vision, and knew that I had just avoided getting hit by inches. I didn't care. The smell was overpowering, and the glowing lines fusing together and breaking apart like a DNA strand. My eyes were locked on it, and I dodged pedestrians and other obstacles, not even stumbling as I followed my goal.

I have no idea how far I ran. The world around me was blurred and out of focus, save for the red light. All I know is that my foot slipped on leaf-sodden pavement mid sprint, and I fell, sprawling across the pavement.

My vision cleared. The scarlet light flickered, then dissipated. The scent left my nostrils. For a full minute, I lay, stunned, on the pavement. Finally, I sat up, wincing at the sudden pain in my leg. I must have pulled a ligament when I fell. Shakily, I got to my feet, and studied my surroundings.

I found that I had not strayed far from where I had started out, only about a block. For a second, I was relieved, glad that I had not gotten lost inside the city. Then I realized where I was, and why the red light trail was the exact color of blood.

Because it was.

I was standing in front of the local hospital.

14

I would *love* to say that when I stood up in front of the hospital, my leg aching and my neck throbbing, I showed restraint, dusted myself off, and said, "Well, what a funny coincidence. I sure am glad I'm not a vampire," and walked away normally.

That was *not* what happened.

A horrid, wrenching nausea pulled at my stomach, and, almost against my own will, I began to run towards the hospital. Every nerve in my body was yelling, no, roaring at me to continue, to run inside, to kill, to *mutilate* every single body in sight, to bite down on the soft flesh of a human, taste the bone marrow and muscle in their neck, and feel their warm blood cascade down my throat...

I had completely lost control. I gripped the metal door handle, sweat dripping into my eyes, my vision swathed in a hazy red. I licked my teeth, feeling the serrated edges of my fangs against my tongue. Saliva dripped in slippery threads from my mouth, and I began to pull the door open.

Just as I prepared to enter the building, an oppressive weakness washed over me. I felt like I had not slept in years. I could barely stay standing. I stumbled backwards, and then a horrid, burning pain exploded in my back, like my coat had burst into flames. Turning, I shielded my eyes from the blinding orange light of the setting sun, and Morton's words came back to me in my head.

Stay out of the sunlight.

I stumbled back, all thoughts of blood gone from my head. My coat was definitely smoldering now, and the burning feeling crept up my legs, like a growing flame. In a panic, I watched in horror as the tips of my fingers began to crumble into dust.

A scream escaped my lips. I ran from the hospital, back across the blocks, the burning feeling growing worse, surrounding me like a blanket. It felt like the sun was chasing me away from the hospital, shaking a fiery fist in my wake. I dashed across the street, and my apartment came into view.

I breathed a sigh of relief, then doubled over in pain again as the fiery agony traveled faster. I crossed to my apartment building in five seconds, threw open the door, and leaped inside.

I was welcomed by the dim light of the lobby. A few residents sat in comfy chairs, reading and sipping coffee. Some of them looked up when I entered, but I barely noticed. As soon as I got out of the sunlight, the agony began to ebb away. My breathe came out in ragged gasps as I leaned against the wall. Holding up my hand, I found that it was still smoldering slightly, and I was fairly certain that humans weren't supposed to smell like cooked meat.

The crumbling effect the sun had had on my fingers seemed to have reversed, but when I tried to bend them, I found that I couldn't. It was like my fingers had been super-glued in place.

I shuddered as I began the stair ascent back to my room. It was not so much the fact that even the *setting* sunlight had harmed me, had almost reduced me to a pile of ashes, that scared me. No, what truly created a pit of dark dread in my stomach was the fact that I was transforming quicker. There could be no other explanation, no doubt about it.

I closed my apartment door with a slam, then I closed the blinds, shutting out the sun. The room darkened, and I rubbed my hand along my aching forehead. Everything had happened too fast. I could still smell burned coat as I got up to make myself coffee. As I eased myself down in a chair, the steaming mug in my hand, I thought over what had happened.

The sun almost seemed to have *targeted* me when I was about to enter the hospital. I remembered Morton's online article, saying that vampires could disintegrate or even explode when coming into contact with sunlight. Far less had happened to me.

I realized that I had avoided certain death by mere minutes.

I opened my mail on my laptop. I scrolled past the ten emails from Maria, then clicked on *compose*. I typed in Morton's email address, and wrote,

Dr. Morton,

You said I should contact you if anything concerning my condition turned up. Unfortunately, in the wake of current events, I have seen fit to inform you of my rapidly deteriorating condition.

Tonight, as I was taking a short stroll, I was seized by a horrid, overpowering desire for blood. I "followed my nose," you could say, to the local hospital. Fear not, I did not attack anyone, though I was very nearly about to. As I prepared to enter the hospital, the

rays of the setting sun washed over me. I take it you can guess what happened. I barely evaded death, and even as I write this, my hand is still smoldering slightly. Please get back to me with my blood tests and your diagnosis as soon as possible. I fear that my transformation is taking major effect. If it is truly irreversible, tell me what I need to do to keep my loved ones safe.

J.H. Henning

I watched the message move to my sent box, and then I closed the laptop. As I leaned back, my eyes began to feel heavy, and my back felt tender and raw against the chair. Once again, I felt completely drained of energy. Maybe I would just sleep until I got Morton's answer, wake up tomorrow...

To go to Maria's place.

I sat bolt upright.

Damn it!

After today's events, I would never have even *considered* going over to Maria's apartment. But I had promised her I would come. Of course, that was *before* I had gone insane with bloodlust. I could not imagine Maria's reaction if I bailed on her. Also, it was growing hard enough not being able to see her on a daily basis.

I sighed. It wouldn't do to not go. I would only regret it later on, if anything happened to me, and I never saw her again. Never got the chance to say goodbye...

That stiffened my resolve. I decided I was going to go, if anything to catch Maria up on my current condition. After that... well, hopefully she'd understand. Her life was in danger every second she spent with me. I am *not* going to hurt her.

15

I have found that, in times of great stress, writing can relieve some of the tension one is feeling. Which is why I've been writing non-stop, all day long today.

On, off, on, off, from this diary to my book and back again. I went on a "writing spree" some might call it. I plowed through the rest of my book, not bothering to consult my notes or thoughts. When I finished, the triumphant 295-page mark glowed at the bottom of my screen. But as I made to send it to my editor, I hesitated.

Strangely, I did not feel a large sense of accomplishment. More than that, I felt shameful. If I had not taken that fateful trip the Romania, all to write a *mediocre novel*, I would never have been attacked by a vampire. I wouldn't be putting Maria in danger.

Pushing *those* cheery thoughts out of my head, I closed the laptop without sending it to my editor, and started on my diary. As I write this now, the pages are rapidly filling up. Maybe I'll need a new one soon. I never considered writing in it after my trip, but now my entries are written almost daily. As I reread it, I was struck by how much it revolved around the horrific events of the past few weeks. Ha! It would appear that my diary makes a better vampire novel than the actual one.

...

I had waited (with good reason) for the sun to set before I hailed a taxi to take me to Maria's. Now the only lights were those of street lamps and the distant glow of Times Square, illuminating the city from the inside like a jack-o-lantern. It was beautiful... but alien at the same time. In all my life in New York City, I had never seen complete darkness, and I doubt I ever will. There was always a headlight, or a street lamp, or a building, with its windows glowing like eyes.

So as the taxi weaved through traffic and cars, I settled back in my seat and closed my eyes, letting the comforting darkness wash over me. I welcomed it, the tranquility of the dark and the gentle rocking of the cab began to lull me to sleep...

And then a familiar, coppery smell wafted to my nose. My head snapped up, every sense on fire. The cab had stopped behind a line of cars, and as I heard the distant wail of an ambulance speeding to the scene, I realized why, with a jolt of dread.

There had been a car crash. Not unheard of in New York, but saliva began to drip from my mouth onto the leather seat of the cab as I stared with hunger as the victim was pulled out of the car. He was almost unrecognizable, so covered in blood I could hardly see his face. But I knew he was alive, because his faint pulse resonated in my ears, still pumping blood to his heart...

I clawed at the door of the cab, but it was locked. I pounded on the sliding door separating me from my driver, but it, too, was closed shut. "LET ME OUT!" I screamed, but he had his radio blasting too high to hear me. I slid down in my seat, cursing with defeat as the victim of the crash was loaded onto the ambulance. The coppery smell left, but I did not feel weak. For the first time since I was attacked in Romania, I felt angry about losing a meal of blood. A sense of cold fury settled upon me, and I ran my tongue along the serrated edges of my teeth.

Soon, I thought darkly, as Maria's apartment came into view, my anger replaced by a deadly sense of peace, like the calm before the storm. Very soon, I am going to feast.

16

Maria opened the door to her apartment after my first knock. Dark circles ringed her eyes, and if I hadn't been suppressing the urge to bite her neck then and there, I would have felt bad. I really *hadn't* contacted her at all. She probably hadn't slept for the past week.

Without a word, she guided me into her apartment, to a chair facing a roaring fire. I didn't feel the heat. I barely felt her touch. All I could hear was her pounding blood in my head. Pulling up a seat across from me, she took my hands in hers and looked searchingly into my eyes. I stared back, trying not to pay attention to the hunger in my stomach. I did not see Maria sitting across from me anymore. All I saw was my first meal.

Finally, she spoke. "James, you didn't call. You didn't text. You cut off all contact with me. Whatever happened at that appointment, you shouldn't"-

"Shhh." I put a finger to her lips, hiding my razor canines from her view in a reassuring smile. "The doctor said I was fine. It was just a small infection, nothing to worry about. He prescribed me something, and sent me on my way. I'm fine. Really."

The lie came so easily, perhaps we were both a little surprised. Silence for another minute, then Maria threw her arms around me. She buried her face in the folds of my shirt, and I realized she was sobbing.

"I-if you had c-caught-something *terminal,* a-and you hadn't told me, and y-you had gone without me s-saying goodbye..."

"There, there," I crooned, putting my arms around her. "It's all right, Maria, I'll be okay," I said, stroking her back soothingly.

I'll be better when I bite out your throat, I thought, but I kept my thoughts to myself.

I wiped the tears off her cheeks. "I'm sure we can do something that can make both of us feel better."

Taking Maria's hand, we walked into her bedroom. Just like my living room, it, too, was stacked with books of many variety, but I didn't notice. With one hand on Maria's back, I eased her onto the bed, without a hint of breath. I was preparing to pounce on my prey.

Maria relaxed under me, and I knew she felt safe. And why wouldn't she? I was fine, no illness, I had come over at last, and I still loved her beyond compare. The thought that those things were true almost made me laugh out loud, but I suppressed it as I turned her over to reveal her neck.

All other thoughts left my head. I was aware that Maria was kissing me, but all my attention was focused on her throat. Leaning down, I traced my tongue along her lower jaw, until I found the deliciously throbbing pulse. My mouth opened wide, wider than I knew it could go, and I struck.

Maria arched her back and screamed. Whether it was out of surprise or pain, I didn't know. And I didn't care. I grabbed her arms, pinning her to the bed as the first drops of blood began to fall.

It was the most nourishing thing I had ever tasted. The hunger vanished the second the first crimson droplet hit my tongue. I cannot describe the sensation. It was like being on the most powerful, most energy-giving drug there was. I bit harder, and a stream of blood showered down my throat.

Maria clawed at me desperately, moaning weakly, "James... stop... please... you're hurting me..."

I didn't stop. I lapped up the flow of blood with my tongue, then sunk my teeth in again. Maria's screams reached falsetto pitch. My teeth slid in deeper. If I had bitten her jugular vein, I would have killed her in a heartbeat. I didn't care. I drank until my stomach was full, then I relented.

Maria stumbled back from me, clutching her neck, blood oozing between her fingers, her face ashen, a look of pure horror and fear on her features. I could feel the dark red liquid dripping off my chin, and I suppressed the urge to lick it off as I sat there, waiting for her to speak.

"What the *fuck* did you just do? James, you attacked me!" she gave a high, disbelieving laugh and sat on her desk. "I mean, you *bit* me? What the *fuck?*"

Her voice was rising, and I said nothing to calm her down. Maria covered her face and broke down in tears, shaky, heavy sobs that made her shoulders shake. And finally, I came out of my trance.

I heard her crying. I could smell the coppery smell of blood. And, with a stab of realization and horror, I realized that I had attacked the woman I had striven so hard to protect.

I leapt off the bed, but she shoved me away. "Get back! Just go, okay? Whatever is happening to you, you could have demonstrated a little less violently! I don't need you to go all Bella Lugosi on me again. Wait..."

Her eyes widened in understanding. "The vampire specialist you told me about. Your pale skin. You bit my neck... oh god. Oh my god. You're a..."

I spread my hands.

"Yes. I didn't want to come into contact with you for the very reason of what I just did. The doctor- George Morton, I can give you his email- diagnosed me with the symptoms of a vampire at the appointment. He told me not to come into contact with those I love, but..."

"No." Maria backed farther away. "No. James, you're the horror *novelist*, not the horror *monster!*"

"Maria," I pleaded, "You've been bitten. I'm not fully transformed, otherwise you would become a vampire, but we still have to get you to Doctor Morton"-

Maria stepped forward and slapped me.

"Don't give me that shit, Dracula. I'm fine. Just get out of my house. Now."

My face stung. With a sob, Maria tore past me, out of the room. I heard the apartment door slam behind her a few seconds later.

I let myself out.

17

Now who was the one not returning calls?

Three days after the attack, Maria still hadn't called, or answered my messages. Understandably, of course, but it still put me into a depression. Since my drink of blood, I had not left my apartment. I had not written, eaten, or slept. Sleep was eluding me more and more every day. I found myself pumped full of energy at night, and drained and exhausted during the day.

And the hunger for blood had returned.

The thing was, I welcomed it. It took every last bit of willpower to not leave my apartment in search of fresh "food," and when the urge got too strong, I would rake my nails along the walls in insane, lustful torment, leaving deep marks in my wake.

This morning, I woke up at six in a cold sweat, clutching the sheets tightly in my hands. The nightmare I had just had faded slowly from my head, but it still left me shivering. The dream had no images in it, just the haunting, high-pitched scream of a woman in agony.

Wiping perspiration off my forehead, I climbed out of bed and stumbled into the bathroom, following the scratch marks I had made the day before on the wall. *You, Mr. Henning, I thought to myself as I turned to the mirror, must look like* a mess.

It turned out I didn't look like anything.

I had no reflection in the mirror. The white wall of the bathroom behind me was all that showed in the reflective glass. No face. No fangs. Nothing. I waved my hand in front of the mirror. Not even a shadow. I would have been unnerved, but this had become the norm for me. If I had turned into a bat right then, I would have said, "Like I didn't see *this* coming."

I had completely given up. I had accepted my cursed fate. Maybe I could have just sat in the sunlight and waited to disintegrate. That certainly would have saved me from what I did that night.

...

As the darkness of night began to take New York once again, I found an email from George Morton waiting for me on my laptop.

Mr. Henning,

I received your email. Apologies for not responding quicker. I have been busy here with your blood sample, and only just finished the final tests. Your letter concerns me, but it is expected, considering your final results. I do not wish to convey them over email, better, I will come to your apartment today, and give them to you in person. In the meantime, continue to stay away from all whom you love.

George A. Morton

Coming...

Here?

I slammed the computer shut. No time to warn him. No time to run. The sun was just beginning to set, but already the sensation of bloodlust was beginning to fill me, invading my senses, bewitching my thoughts.

A steady rain began to fall, making light *plink, plink, plink* noises on the apartment building roof. I pulled back the curtains, sunlight be damned, and witnessed a sleek, black car pull up next to the building.

Morton. Oh, my god.

Even from three stories up, I could smell the blood inside the vial he was carrying in a briefcase as he stepped out of the car. My test results.

My own blood. He was about to deliver his diagnosis, but I didn't need it to know what I had become.

I threw open the window, and leaned out, the rain hitting my face in the gusts of the wind. "GEORGE!" I yelled through the rain, "TURN BACK!"

Morton looked up through the rain, his coat blowing behind him, shielding his eyes from the water, which was now coming down in torrents. He shook his head, indicating he hadn't heard me through the wind.

I cupped my hands over my mouth and positively screamed, "I TRANSFORMED ALREADY! IT'S TOO LATE! GO BACK NOW, WHILE YOU CAN! I'M A"-

The rest of my words were lost on the wind, which hit me with a wave of screaming air. I was aware of my feet leaving the rain soaked carpet, felt myself lean just a *little* too far out, and the next thing I knew, I was falling, almost in slow motion, out the window, straight towards Morton. Through the rain I saw his eyes widen in shock, and then I was back in the Black Forest, looking through someone else's eyes; I was falling silently from a tree branch, my teeth bared, staring with hunger at the puny figure below me.

I flashed back to reality as I hit the ground, sending rainwater flying in every direction. Not a single bone broken. Not even a scratch. Slowly, I raised my head and stared at Morton, saliva mixing with the rain on my face. He was coming forward, his face fearful but determined. He was fumbling for something silver attacked to a chain around his neck. A crucifix.

With a snarl, I launched myself through the air, barreling into Morton with all my force. With a grunt of surprise, Morton stumbled, then fell on the rain-sodden street, the cross snapping from its chain and skittering into a gutter.

Morton turned just as I bore down on him again. His hands found my neck as I lunged, and for a minute, we silently struggled on the cold ground, him trying to push me away, and me trying to rip out his windpipe. For a second, it appeared that Morton was going to pull me off of him.

But the fact that a vampire's strength is double that of a man's won out. With a roar of triumph, I shoved Morton's hands away and sunk my teeth as deep as they could go into his neck.

Morton howled. His body twitched, then went completely slack. He had died almost instantly. By then, I had turned manic. I locked my teeth under the skin on his neck and pulled. Blood exploded out of his neck as I peeled the skin away with a ripping noise, showering the street in red and splattering my face. The torn muscle and sinew hung like limp fingers from

the destroyed inside of his neck.
Morton's hand twitched once more,
then was still.

...

Say what you will about vampires.
We clean up after ourselves.

I slurped up the blood from the
wound until there was no more to
drink. Or maybe it was the effect of
my spit. I once heard that a vampire
bat's saliva clots the wound of their
victims, stemming the flow of blood,
so I suppose that's what happened here.

Finally, when the wound had been
sucked dry of the last drop of blood,
I straightened up and wiped my mouth
on my sleeve. Darkness had completely
fallen now, but my bloodlust had been
sated for the night. I didn't bother to

move Morton's corpse either. It would be found soon enough anyway. I felt a twinge of pity, however, as I looked at Morton, propped on the side of his car, the shiny black metal smeared with blood. He had come to help me, after all.

Well, I thought as I strode back into the apartment, his loss.

18

When I entered my apartment again, my hand leaving Morton's blood smeared on the doorknob, I immediately knew someone else was inside. It is the presence you can't see but can *feel*, like someone is watching you.

It appeared I was to have a two course meal that night.

I was so pumped with the energy that Morton's blood had given me that it was hard to not make noise. Silently, I walked through the kitchen, wiping my hands on my shirt as I did so. Best not to alarm my victim until after I tore them apart.

Was I not thinking straight? Duh. I had just killed a man. Was I in the mood for second helpings? Yes. So, with a snarl that sounded more beast than man, I leapt into the living room, my hands raised like claws, and came face to face with...

Maria.

All the energy drained out of me and was replaced with the exhaustion of a man who had not slept in a week. My hands dropped to my side. Maria's eyes flicked from the wet blood on my chin to my blood-stained shirt. "Maria," I began, prepared to tell another lie, "This isn't what it looks"-

She cut me off. "Don't start, James. I know already. I saw it all. I called Morton and we agreed to meet

at your apartment. You know...
strength in numbers."

It suddenly struck me that
Morton hadn't just come to give me the
results. He had come to restrain me
from doing what I had done to him
just a few minutes ago. A surge of
guilt washed over me for the first
time.

"But you got to Morton first. At
the last second he told me to run, that
he could handle you, but... I can see
that he was in over his head." She
gestured to my blood-stained clothes.
"After that, I fled into your apartment,
and... here I am."
I knew she was thinking and *I'm not
dead... yet.*

I backed away from her, like *she* was the bloodsucking demon in the room. Like *she* was the monster. "Maria"- my voice caught in my throat. "You may have killed yourself by coming here. I-I've lost control."

Maria shook her head. "No. we're going to get you help, James, you just need to"-

I finally lost it. "Don't you get it? I've had a *death* sentence on my head since September! I've been *crumbling*, getting hit over and over and over and over by this damnable transformation. I have stopped writing. I have stopped seeing you. Even though I'm not dead, I'm not *living* anymore. This curse has been around for centuries, and I can't reverse it. You saw what happened to the one man who could help me. Be glad he's dead, instead of slowly being infected, slowly dying like I am..."

My voice trailed off. I sunk to the ground, all energy gone. I did not cry easily, but tears streamed freely from my eyes now. I felt Maria kneel next to me, and then next thing I knew, her forehead was against mine, and she was crying as well, her tears mixing with mine. For a few minutes, we just sat on the floor, holding each other, shaking with sobs at the cruel, cruel nature of the world.

...

Finally, Maria pulled back, and spoke, in a shaky, tired voice, "I can't save you. You're right. But you are still the man I love. And I can stand with you until you can't stand anymore. And then I will still be with you. No matter what happens."

I leaned over and brushed back the hair from her face. "I know. If I transform tomorrow, my life still would have been worth something. Because you are in it." I tried for a confident smile, but on the inside, thoughts were racing at top speed through my head. *I won't be transforming tomorrow, though. I won't kill ever again. I'm going to make sure of it. But you can't be with me where I'm going.*

19

The simplicity of death really is astounding. One minute, you are on earth, *living* your life, the next second... *boom*. Gone.

Those were the thoughts going through my head as I write this down. In one hand, I hold this pen, scribbling my last notes. In the other, I hold a wooden stake of oak.

Yes. Say what you will, but this is the solution. Stay alive and almost definitely guarantee Maria's death, and the deaths of other innocents in New York City, or end the true horror before it begins. Live as an undead husk of my former self, or die, and save all around me.

My mind was made up, you can see.

Talk about multitasking. It's ironic that my own vampire strength is going to help me put this stake in my chest. But I do not fear death. I have been living in its folds for weeks. And even as I feel the burning pain of it lodging through my heart, I am still writing this last entry. Books were such a big part of my life, it is fitting that I die after making just one more. I

am going to die as I lived. Writing-

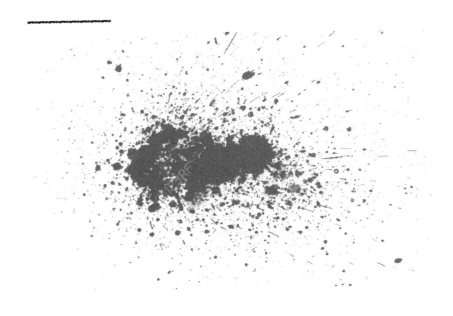

20

Steve Osborn finished reading the last sentence and stared at the dark, dried brown blood spattered across the page. He closed the blue book in a state of shock, barely able process what he had just read.

A vampire.

Hours before, when Osborn had sat down at his desk, the diary unread, he would never have believed it. But now, as he stared at that last, blood-soaked page, he was having second thoughts. He flipped through the diary and pulled out the note from the deceased author.

To Whom It May Concern:

By the time you find this letter, I will already be dead. Believe me, it is for the best. I am no longer a danger to myself and to those around me. This letter is enclosed in my diary. Read it if you want answers to what has happened to me. But be warned: you will not believe any of it at first.

Damn right I wouldn't have believed it, thought Osborn as he read the rest.

The experiences that led me to this act are none for the faint of heart, and I beg for you to understand my decision. After you read my final writings, all will be made clear. Do not pity me in my plight, in doing this act I save the lives of all who live in New York City.

But how could you *not* pity someone with so cruel a fate? Osborn realized that Henning wasn't asking for pity. He was pleading for forgiveness.

If you are reading this, and you are not Maria Bennet, please see that this letter and the news of my death reach her. Give her all of my love.

James Henry Henning

Osborn frowned. Henning hadn't provided Ms. Bennet's address in his letter. Nevertheless, Osborn saw the request that the letter reach Ms. Bennet as James Henning's final wish. He intended to see it through, even if Henning really had been a…

Osborn shuddered and stared out the window at the dark night. He cursed the fact that morning was still hours away, and convinced himself that he would feel better when daylight illuminated New York once more. Still, after reading that chilling diary, he couldn't shake the feeling that he was being watched.

Stop it, he told himself. *Get your mind off of vampires. Think about how much trouble you're going to be in when the chief finds out you kept evidence…*

Damn. Osborn had been so sucked into the diary, he had forgotten that he had technically stolen it from the crime scene. Maybe he could find some way to sneak it into the evidence room. If the chief found out he had taken it, his fate was going to be worse than Henning's…

A sudden, terrifying idea blossomed in Osborn's mind. It sent a cold, foreboding feeling down his spine. He ran back to his desk and flipped through the diary, searching frantically for the right entry. He finally found it, written in Henning's untidy scrawl. It was the list of vampire traits the author had taken from the internet.

From Morton.

The vampire specialist had been brutally murdered by Henning, killed by his own line of work. According to the diary, the only witnesses had been James's girlfriend and the author himself, who, according to his diary, had committed the felony under the uncontrollable bloodlust of a vampire.

Trying, and failing, to push those thoughts out of his head, Osborn scrolled his finger down the page, searching for the one fact that would confirm his deepest fears.

Sunlight... no...

Wooden stakes... Henning used *those* to their full extent...

Crucifix... good luck with that, Morton...

Suicide... here we go...

- SUICIDE: if a human, infected already or not, commits suicide, he or she is reanimated as a vampire

Osborn's blood ran cold. The image of Henning, a stake through his chest, lying dead on the living room floor flashed back to him. The author's final letter, stating his choice of killing himself, fluttered to the ground at Osborn's feet.

Henning hadn't prevented his vampire fate.

In taking his own life, he had completed it.

A feeling of total dread took hold of him. He put the note back in the diary and snapped it shut just as he heard heavy footfalls mounting the stairs to his office. Whoever was coming up the creaking wooden old staircase was doing it slowly, like they had all the time in the world.

It's the chief, he tried to reassure himself. *He wants to know if I found any more evidence. I'll just give it to him and accept the consequences. No use hiding anything... it's just the chief. It's just the chief.*

The staircase squeaked again, and Steve finally sprang up and locked the door with a key. *Boss be damned,* he thought, *I'm not taking any chances with that bastard blood-drinker out there.*

The footfalls stopped outside the door. Osborn drew in a breath, waiting. Whoever it was had ceased all noise. For a minute, the silence was the loudest thing in the room. Then, with a click that seemed to resound in Osborn's ears, the doorknob wiggled and turned. The lock had been broken.

Osborn's hand was now on his pistol, but he was too petrified with fear to take it out of its holster. He watched in mute horror as the door opened.

The thing that used to be James Henry Henning entered the room slowly, almost leisurely. His skin was white, almost perfectly so, even whiter than the last time Osborn had seen him. His bulbous, glowing red eyes were so sunken back in their sockets that they seemed to vanish behind a blanket of shadows. Below his white lips, Henning's yellowing fangs protruded like tusks from the top of his mouth, freezing it in a permanent snarl. Against the stark pallor of his face, his black hair seemed to blend into the darkness around him. In the center of his chest, a gaping, black hole yawned wide open, with dry blood crusted around it. The stake had been pulled out.

Henning stepped into the room, surveying his surroundings with those demonic eyes. His gaze locked onto him, and another chill coursed through Osborn's body. He felt like a deer, not sure of what was about to happen to it, right before the hunter put a bullet in its head.

The thought of bullets jogged him back to reality. Osborn was a hardened vet. He wasn't going down without a fight. Whipping his gun out of its holster, he pointed it at the vampire's face. In his other hand, he held tightly to the diary, his hand growing slippery with sweat.

"James Henning." He spoke the words almost like a curse, an insult reserved for the lowest of the low.

The creature raised a pale hand and studied it, almost curiously. His eyes flickered dangerously "Yes," he said in a completely human voice. It was scarier than if he had opened his mouth and growled at Osborn. "I was him once. In another life."

Osborn fought to keep his voice calm. "Listen, James. I read your diary just now. I know what happened. We can help you. Just let me notify"–

"Ah, yes," Henning purred, "My diary. I almost forgot what I was here for."

Faster than the gunshot that Osborn fired blindly through the wide hole in Henning's chest, the author sprang across the room and secured the chief detective's neck in the crook of his arm. His hot, rank breath smelled like rotting flesh as he spoke in a near whisper.

"As much as your concern and offer to help touches me, I'm afraid I must turn it down. But don't worry, officer," Henning breathed the last words, filled with malice, into Osborn's ear, "You won't have to worry about *anything* ever again."

Effortlessly, the author snapped Osborn's head to the side in one quick movement. Osborn's last, final thought as he hit the ground was a prayer of thanks, that it had ended so quickly. No bite. Just darkness.

...

Henning was disappointed. No blood had been spilt. He would have to find some other way to sate his hunger that night. Ah, well. It didn't matter. He had a whole city of victims to choose from.

Henning bent down and plucked the diary out of Osborn's limp hand. He intended, of course, to destroy it as quickly as possible. The story of what had happened to him was a good way to warn the people of New York City to his presence. And he couldn't have that. If that happened, it would be much harder to achieve his goal of infecting every last soul in this city.

Well…

Every soul but one.

I haven't forgotten you, Maria Bennet, thought the vampire, staring out at the dark city before him, *and I never will. Not in life…*

A cruel smile played across his white face.

Or in death.

About the author

Charlie Williams is an aspiring teen author. Since childhood, he has been fascinated with the subject of horror. So far in his writing career, he has written five books in the genre: *The Son of Krueger, The Demon in the Dark, Krueger's Legacy, Scarecrow,* and his latest, *The Final Entries of J.H. Henning.* Williams lives in Virginia with his family.

66313433R00090

Made in the USA
Charleston, SC
14 January 2017